Discover Series
Kitchen

COCINA

Licuadora

Blender

Abrelatas

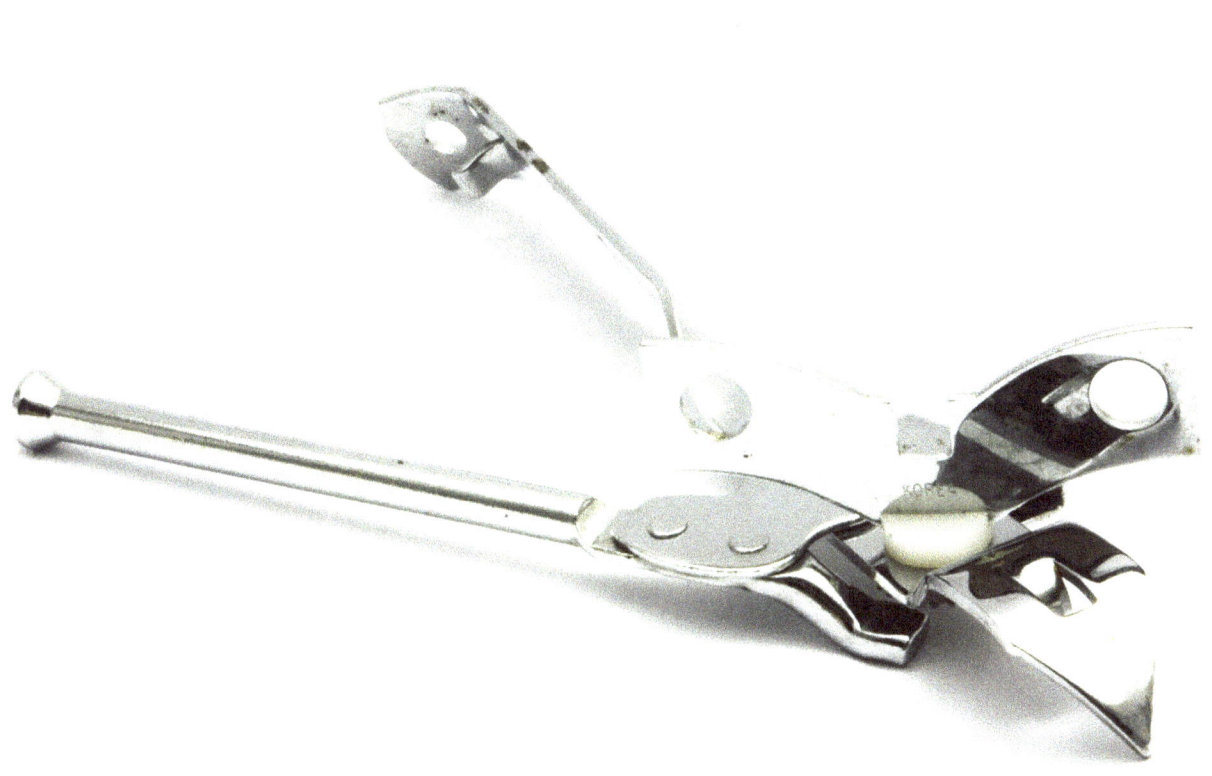

Can Opener

Rallador de Queso

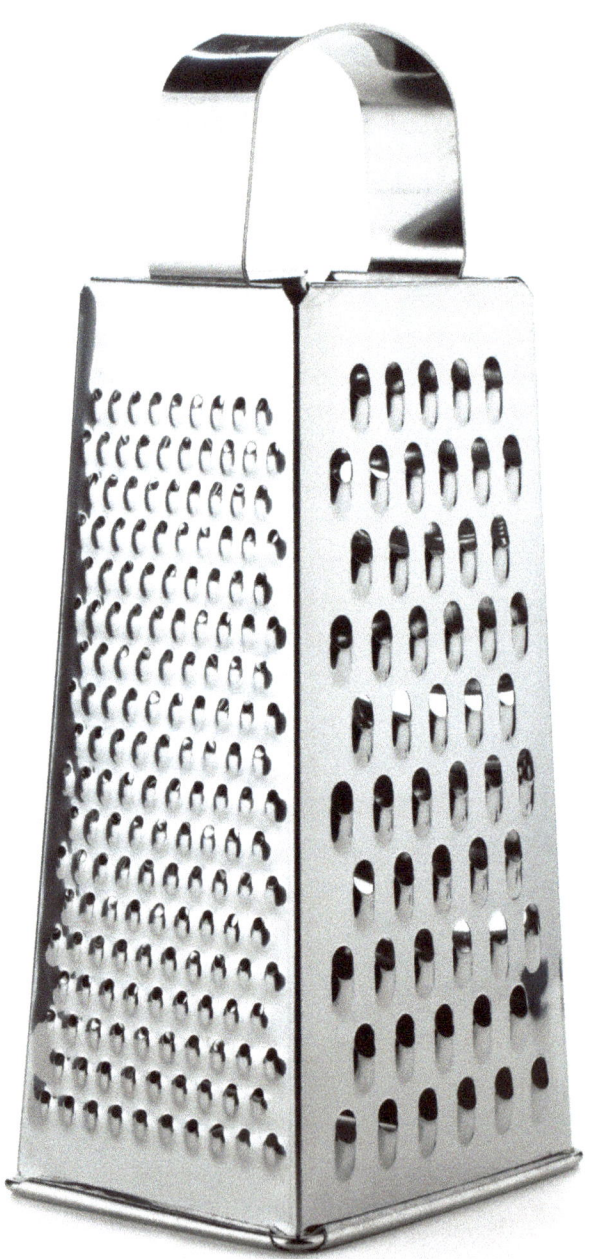

Cheese Grater

Palillos

Chop Sticks

Tazas de Café

Coffee Mugs

Utensilios de Cocina

Cooking Utensils

Jabon para Trastes

Dish Soap

Lavaplatos

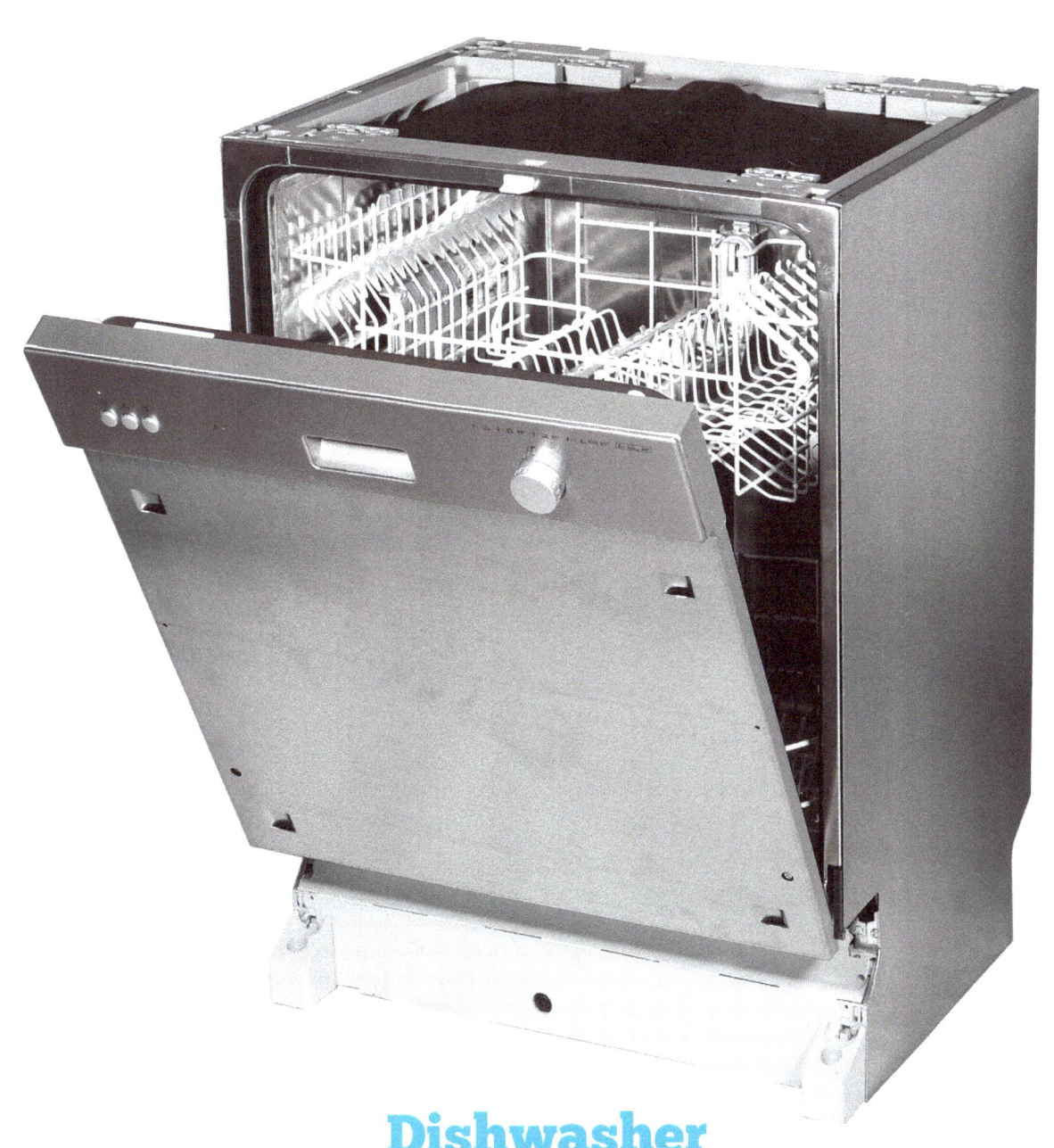

Dishwasher

Hervidor Eléctrico

Electric Kettle

Procesador de Alimentos

Food Processor

Tenedor, Cuchara y Cuchillo

Fork, Spoon and Knife

Sarten

Frying Pan

Cuchillo de Cocina

Kitchen Knife

Peso de Cocina

Kitchen Scale

Microondas

Microwave

Aceite de Olivo

Olive Oil

Contenedores de Plástico

Plastic Containers

Ollas y Sartenes

Pots and Pans

Refrigerador

Refrigerator

Olla Arrocera

Rice Cooker

Rodillo

Rolling Pin

Ensaladera

Salad Bowl

Salero

Salt Shaker

Tostadora

Toaster

Jarra de Agua

Water Pitcher

Make Sure to Check Out the Other Discover Series Books from Xist Publishing:

Published in the United States by Xist Publishing
www.xistpublishing.com
PO Box 61593 Irvine, CA 92602

© 2018 by Xist Publishing All rights reserved
Translated by Victor Santana
No portion of this book may be reproduced without express permission of the publisher
All images licensed from Fotolia
First Bilingual Edition

ISBN: 978-1-5324-0667-6   eISBN: 978-1-5324-0668-3

xist Publishing

www.ingramcontent.com/pod-product-compliance
Lightning Source LLC
LaVergne TN
LVHW070950070426
835507LV00030B/3479